Walt Disney's

MICKEY MOUSE

MY LIFE IN PICTURES

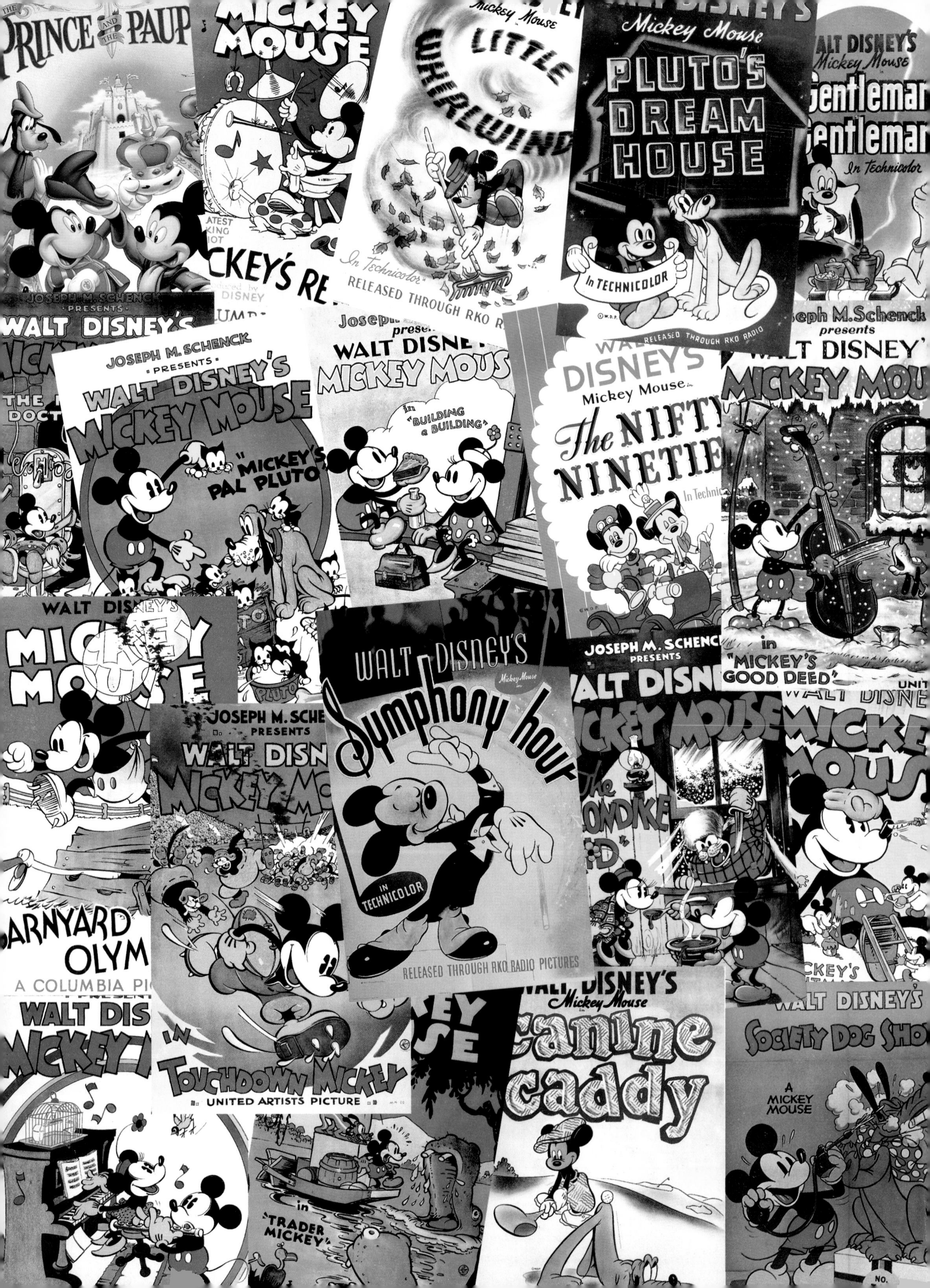

THE PRINCE AND THE PAUP
MICKEY MOUSE
CKEY'S RE
Mickey Mouse
LITTLE WHIRLWIND
In Technicolor
RELEASED THROUGH RKO R
WALT DISNEY'S
Mickey Mouse
PLUTO'S DREAM HOUSE
In TECHNICOLOR
RELEASED THROUGH RKO RADIO
WALT DISNEY'S
Mickey Mouse
Gentleman
Gentleman
In Technicolor
JOSEPH M. SCHENCK
PRESENTS
WALT DISNEY'S
JOSEPH M. SCHENCK
PRESENTS
WALT DISNEY'S
MICKEY MOUSE
"MICKEY'S PAL PLUTO"
Joseph M. Schenck
presents
WALT DISNEY'S
MICKEY MOUSE
in "BUILDING a BUILDING"
WALT DISNEY'S
Mickey Mouse
The NIFTY NINETIES
In Technicolor
Joseph M. Schenck
presents
WALT DISNEY'S
MICKEY MOUSE
in "MICKEY'S GOOD DEED"
WALT DISNEY'S
MICKEY MOUSE
BARNYARD OLYM
A COLUMBIA PIC
JOSEPH M. SCHE
PRESENTS
WALT DISN
MICKEY MO
IN TOUCHDOWN MICKEY
UNITED ARTISTS PICTURE
WALT DISNEY'S
Mickey Mouse
Symphony hour
IN TECHNICOLOR
RELEASED THROUGH RKO RADIO PICTURES
JOSEPH M. SCHENCK
PRESENTS
WALT DISNE
MICKEY MOUSE
WALT DISNE
MICKEY MOUSE
WALT DIS
MICKEY M
in "TRADER MICKEY"
WALT DISNEY'S
Mickey Mouse
canine caddy
WALT DISNEY'S
SOCIETY DOG SHOW
A MICKEY MOUSE

Walt Disney's
MICKEY MOUSE

MY LIFE IN PICTURES

as told to his good friend
Russell Schroeder

Disney
PRESS

Art Direction by Kenneth Shue

Design by Janice Kawamoto

Copyright © 1997 by Disney Enterprises, Inc.

Printed in the United States of America.

First Edition

10   9   8   7   6   5   4   3   2   1

Artwork in this book are actual animation drawings used in the creation of The Walt Disney Studio's animated films.

This book is set in 14/22 Bauer Bodoni and 11/18 Helvetica Compressed.

Library of Congress Catalog Card Number: 97-66143

ISBN 0-7868-3150-2 (trade)
ISBN 0-7868-5059-0 (lib. bdg.)

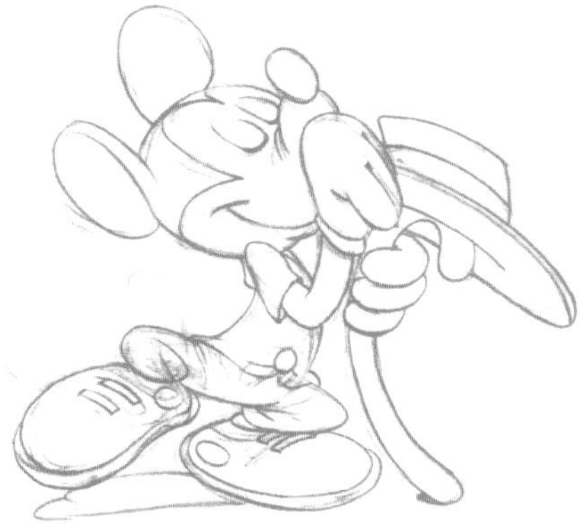

Contents

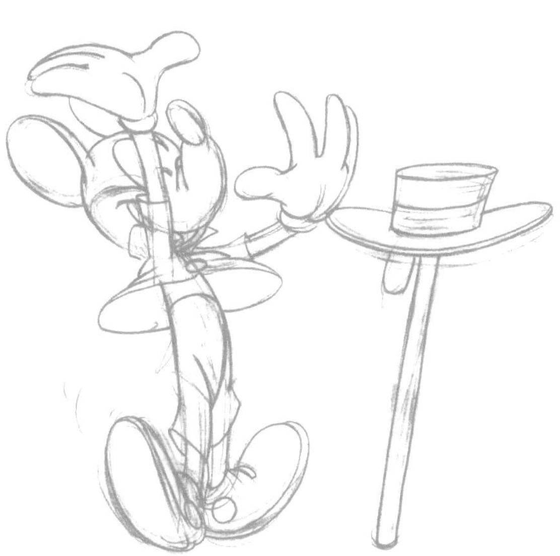

Dear Friends,

 Once, when Walt Disney commented on how much his Studio had grown, he added, "I hope we never lose sight of one thing: that it all started with a mouse." Well, gosh! What a compliment that was to a little guy like me! And now when I look back on all the great things that have happened, the people I've been lucky enough to work with, and all the friends I've made around the world, I just have to say that, for me, "It all started with a man." And that man, of course, was Walt Disney.

Walt and I met on a train ride in 1928. We were both heading west, to California. It was going to be my first visit to that land of orange groves and sunshine–and Hollywood. I was young, filled with hope, and looking for adventure. But I could tell that Walt's mood didn't match mine. You see, he had been making animated films in Hollywood for five years by this time, and he had just learned back in New York that he had lost the contract to his rising new star, Oswald the Lucky Rabbit. This was a severe blow to Walt's small studio, and he didn't know how he'd break the bad news to his partners and coworkers.

I tried to cheer him up, and as we talked, we found we had a lot in common. We both had come from the Midwest and had spent some of our happiest days living on farms near small towns. We both liked to tinker with mechanical objects–to build things. And we were both curious and interested in all the exciting goings-on around us. Right from the start we hit it off like franks 'n' beans.

We chatted for awhile, and then Walt had an idea. He asked me if I had ever thought about going into the movies. Me? What would *I* do? Walt said I was a natural–just a typical, average guy. And some of the adventures I'd been telling him about would make great movie stories, too.

You could have knocked me over with a feather duster, though, when Walt said I should change my name. (A lot of movie stars did that back then.) He suggested I be called–and you can laugh if you want to–Mortimer Mouse! Boy, was I glad Mrs. Disney was there. She saw me kinda wrinkle my brow, and she told Walt that "Mickey" would do just fine.

So, as just plain Mickey Mouse, I arrived at Walt's bustling studio in Hollywood, and I met the men and women who would start me on a long career.

Over the years, many of my friends from back home came to join me at the Disney Studio. And, as Walt and I would often say to each other, it's been a lot of hard work. Sometimes the future faced us with more of a scowl than a smile, but mostly it's been a lot of fun. And I'm glad to have the chance here to relive so many of those great memories. I hope you enjoy reading about them, too.

Your pal,

Mickey

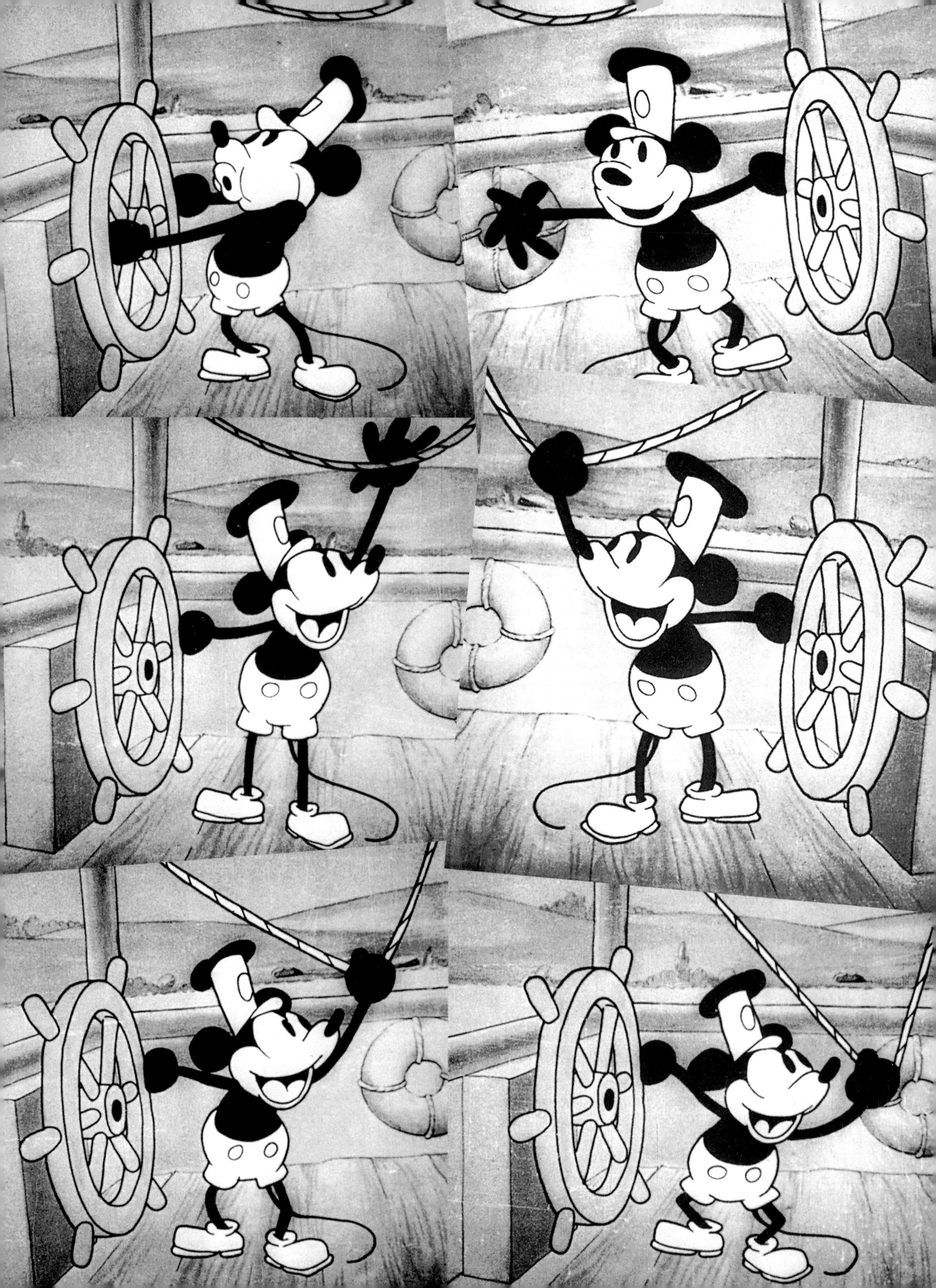

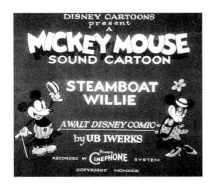

We had the premiere for *Steamboat Willie* at the Colony Theater in New York City on November 18, 1928.

1920s

Folks call it the Jazz Age. Music that throbbed with a toe-tapping rhythm was heard everywhere. And the country seemed to be moving along to that same catchy beat.

Then, in 1927, sound was introduced to the movie industry. Talking pictures! Movies with music and singing!

Walt and I had finished our first two films. They were silent, just like all the other cartoons at that time, and Walt set out to find someone who would distribute them to movie theaters. But our high hopes weren't shared by anybody else in the movie business. No one was interested in Mickey Mouse cartoons! But Walt was convinced that we were a special team. We just needed some way for people to notice us.

We decided to do our third film with sound. Making music has always come naturally to me. You may have noticed that I even walk with a bouncy step, like I'm always hearing a tune in my head. Anyway, we improvised a soundtrack to our film *Steamboat Willie*. And the rest— as they say—is movie history. This was Walt's first great success, and I'm proud as punch that I was a part of it.

Steamboat Willie, 1928

What fun we had making music, using everything from pots and pans to barnyard animals!

The animals were the most unlikely "instruments" anyone could imagine, and audiences howled with laughter.

Minnie's been my sweetheart and costar right from the start. When a goat ate her sheet music, she showed her musical ingenuity, too!

Plane Crazy, 1928

Charles Lindbergh's flight across the Atlantic inspired me to great heights, too. (Only, as it turned out, I came down to earth pretty quickly.)

The Gallopin' Gaucho, 1928

I wonder if Lucky Lindy would have okayed turkey feathers as a rudder for his plane?

Pete relished his role as the "heavy" in our pictures, and we often found ourselves at cross-purposes and crossed swords.

In 1929 our friends Horace Horsecollar and Clarabelle Cow left the farm and joined Minnie and me in Hollywood.

Ub Iwerks was Walt's first business partner and the man mainly responsible for how I looked in my early films.

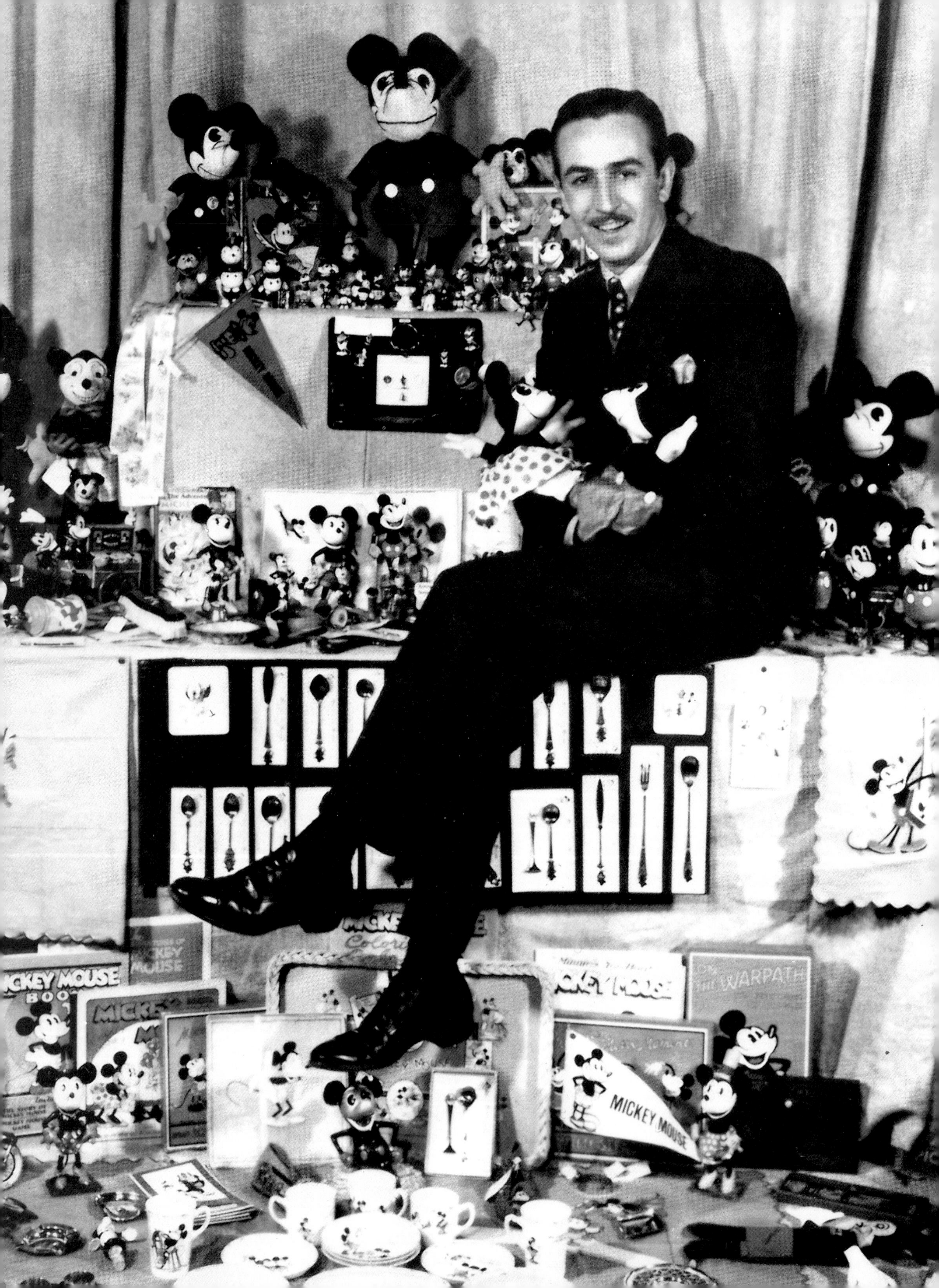
ON THE WARPATH
MICKEY MOUSE

I couldn't believe that Walt had licensed so much merchandise that looked like me! It was enough to fill even the biggest toy chest.

1930s

The Jazz Age of the 1920s came to a close with a bang! But not with a musical crash of cymbals. This crash was the sound of Wall Street stocks tumbling, sending the country into the Great Depression of the 1930s.

This was a hard time for a lot of people, including those of us at the Disney Studio. But we just kept plugging away with our films, and Walt kept experimenting and making them better and better. I like to think that in some small way the pictures that Walt and I made brought a bit of cheer into people's lives. A lot of folks even welcomed Minnie and me and the rest of our pals into their homes in books and as toys and other merchandise. At a time when people were losing their jobs and many businesses were having to close their doors, some manufacturers were saved from bankruptcy and their employees kept on the job by producing Mickey Mouse watches and toys.

Finally the dark skies of the Depression started to disappear, and by the end of the 1930s, Walt had successfully entered the feature-film field and had cast me for a starring role in his most ambitious project to date–*Fantasia!*

I was lucky to have some of the most talented composers in the business creating music for my films. Here, along with Walt, are two of the best—Leigh Harline (left) and Frank Churchill.

Here's a recording session from the early '30s. Unlike today, everything was recorded at the same time back then—music, voices, even sound effects. That kept us all on our toes!

Walt and I wanted the whole Studio to share the honor when he received his first Oscar in 1932 for having started me on my motion picture career.

Walt wrote the stories and Ub Iwerks made the drawings when my newspaper comic first appeared in 1930.

The Chain Gang, 1930

In one of my early films, an infectious *hayuk-yuk* laugh was heard from the audience. Folks have been laughing along with my lovable pal Goofy ever since.

Mickey's Revue, 1932

Pluto didn't even have a name when he was given a bit part in one of my films. Pretty soon, though, he became my best friend and faithful companion.

A volatile volcano of temperament erupted when Donald Duck joined our acting company in 1934! In spite of all his fuss and feathers, though, he's still one of my best pals.

15

I have had a lot of different jobs
in my films!

Neither snow nor sleet (or a bandit named
Pete) kept me from delivering the mail.

Building a Building, 1933

My steam shovel scooped up
gobs of dirt when I was a
construction worker...

...but I tossed that all
aside to go into the box
lunch business with
Minnie.

MICKEY-
MINNIE
BOX
LUNCHES

Donald and I joined those proud
men in blue...

The Dognapper, 1934

...and put the long arm of the law on Pete,
who was up to no good, as usual.

Two-Gun Mickey, 1934

Shucks, Pardner, when a cowpoke sashays up to a sassy filly like Miss Minnie, his heart's gonna go a-poppin' like a six-shooter teched with a brandin' iron. (That's cowboy lingo for "East or West, Minnie's the best!")

One of my favorite jobs has always been leading a band...

The Band Concert, 1935

...even when I have to keep the orchestra together through a tornado!

My pals Goofy and Donald often lent a helping hand on the job. One time we all heeded the siren call and became firefighters.

Mickey's Fire Brigade, 1935

17

Mickey's Polo Team, 1936

Walt's love of playing polo inspired me to put together my own team, and we played against some of Hollywood's biggest stars.

Mickey's Grand Opera, 1936

Clara Cluck gave our musicals a touch of class. When she warbled her operatic arias...

...she brought down the house—literally! Grand opera became grand uproar!

Thru the Mirror, 1936

Mr. Astaire, step aside! My fancy footwork was never better than when I entered a nonsense world just like *Alice in Wonderland*.

Mickey's Circus, 1936

My life was so busy, it often felt like a three-ring circus! So it was only natural to find myself actually in the center ring one day.

19

One of the highest positions in the workforce I ever held was when I joined Goofy and Donald to clean the clock atop the city's tallest skyscraper.

Magician Mickey, 1937

I donned a magician's top hat and silk cape for some nifty sleight-of-hand.

Clock Cleaners, 1937

Lonesome Ghosts, 1937

One of our scariest jobs was as ghost-chasing detectives. *Boo!*

In 1938 Minnie and I got choice roles in an elaborate costume drama, *Brave Little Tailor*.

As the tailor, my boast of "Seven with one blow" (flies, that is) got me in some hot water!

The king appointed me Royal High Killer of the Giant! *Gulp!*

But when Princess Minnie showed such faith in me, how could I refuse?

Once again I proved that size isn't everything— when you can use your brains (and a sturdy needle and thread)!

Brave Little Tailor, 1938

21

Since the spring of 1930, Floyd Gottfredson had taken over as the chronicler of my stories for our newspaper strip. When his talented hand dipped a drawing pen into a bottle of india ink, he brought my most exciting adventures to life.

It took some doing, but Minnie and I eventually clipped the wings of the mysterious Bat Bandit during a trip to a ranch out West.

Printer's ink really is in my blood! For a while, I got to run my own newspaper, *The Daily War Drum.*

On assignment for the Secret Service, I joined the Foreign Legion.

I took the place of my look-alike, King Michael IV, and helped save his throne when a traitorous duke plotted to overthrow the king.

Cast away on a desert island, I met Robinson Crusoe himself.

Chief O'Hara asked me to help solve a baffling crime wave...

...devised by that shadowy villain, The Phantom Blot.

I once found a magic lamp—complete with a not-too-bright genie. Look what happened when I asked him to make my dog Pluto appear!

Over forty years later Floyd was still the main artist for our comic strip!

23

Throughout the '30s, Walt and his staff sent out pictures
of my friends and me on the company's Christmas cards.
We shared our wishes for a joyous holiday season and
a bright, happy New Year.

It's always a welcome change of pace when
I get to slow down, gather my friends, and
wish everyone a time of peace.

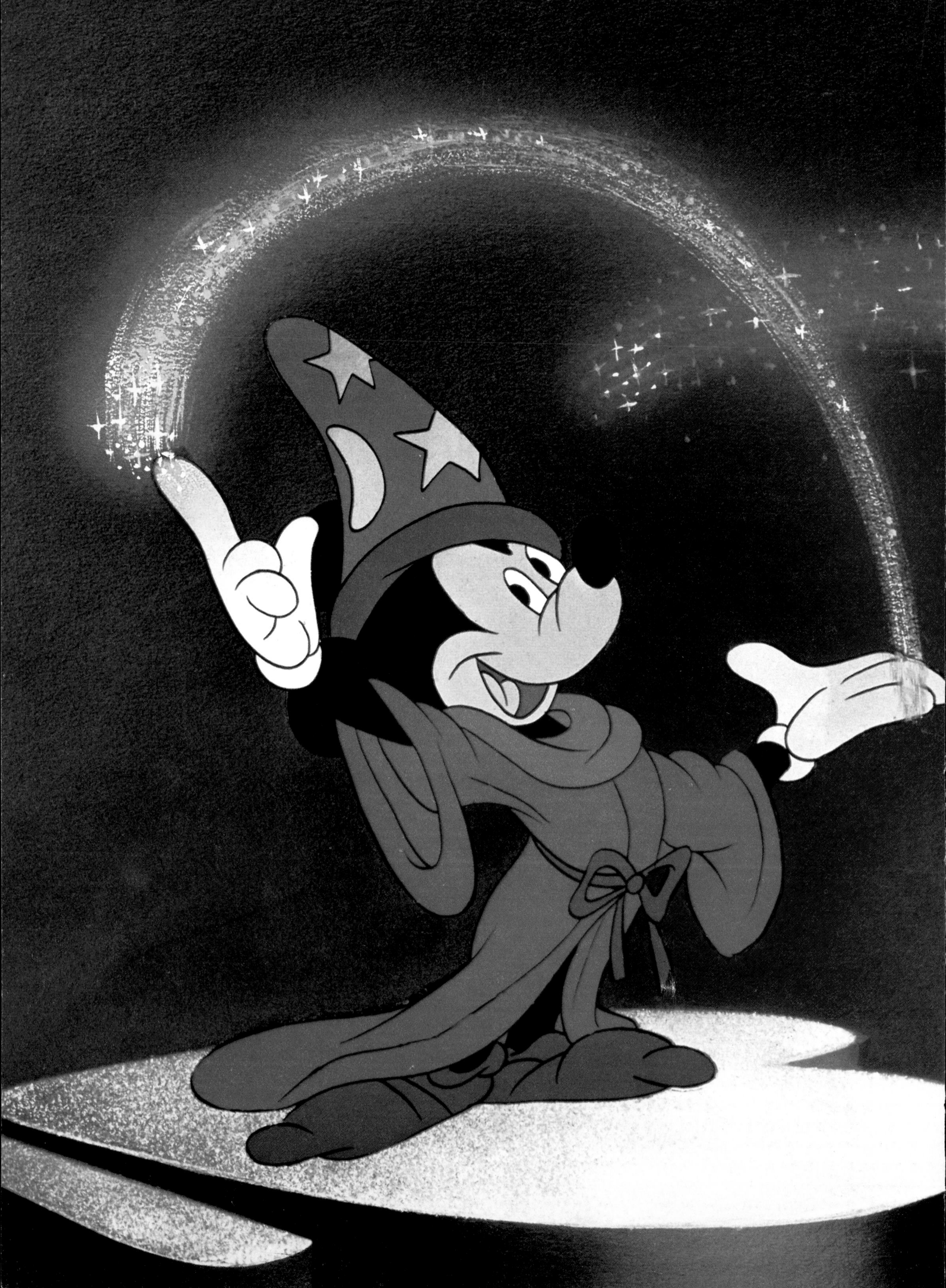

I helped put the finishing touches on the logo that would be used at our new studio.

Pack up the drawing boards...fasten the stoppers in the inkwells...load the cameras...we're moving!

Like the swirling flood waters in the sorcerer's castle in *Fantasia*, our growing staff had filled and overflowed the buildings at the Disney Studio on Hyperion Avenue. So, at the beginning of 1940, with a merry "heigh-ho," we marched over the hills of Hollywood into the peaceful town of Burbank, where Walt had built a brand-new studio.

But while we were marching to our new home in the San Fernando Valley, the world was on the march, too. Sadly, World War II had begun.

Soon the United States had entered the war, and all of us at the Disney Studio joined our friends around the world in the fight for freedom. Our cartoons kept people's spirits up and even helped train our soldiers for the important jobs facing them. We assisted in raising money for the war effort and also served as goodwill ambassadors. It was a busy time, but like all good citizens, we were proud to do our bit.

We were all excited to see the architect's drawing
for the new Disney Studio in Burbank. The buildings
were designed especially for folks working in the
animated cartoon business.

Pluto met one of his future costars on
the set for *Pinocchio*, the first feature
completed at our new studio.

I really threw myself into the role of the unlucky apprentice sorcerer who let loose some magic he couldn't control. Audiences were swept into this story by the thrilling music and exciting special effects. It became one of my most famous roles (and one of my favorites, too).

Fantasia, 1940

The Little Whirlwind, 1941

One time my gardening chores were interrupted by a tiny whirlwind. I thought I had everything under control...

...until his mama breezed onto the scene and almost blew me out of the picture!

Minnie and I always enjoy dressing up in costume for a movie. In *The Nifty Nineties* we portrayed sweethearts from a quieter, simpler era.

Just like sweethearts from that bygone era, we capped off our date with a thrilling ride in a horse-less carriage—at the breathtaking speed of fifteen miles an hour! Back in the 1890s that was fast!

Two of our favorite animators, Ward Kimball and Fred Moore, even entertained *us* during a vaudeville show.

The Nifty Nineties, 1941

Good ol' Pluto! One time he rescued a kitten from drowning. He was rewarded with both my and the kitten's thanks—and the 1941 film we made of his adventure, *Lend A Paw*, won an Academy Award.

Lend A Paw, 1941

Symphony Hour, 1942

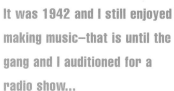

It was 1942 and I still enjoyed making music—that is until the gang and I auditioned for a radio show...

...and the performance almost ended in disaster when all our instruments got broken.

31

Like many of the other stars in Hollywood,
all my pals at the Disney Studio mobilized to
help out with the war effort.

The British Lion watches as we
"stoke the fires" of U.S. aid to our
embattled ally.

What an honor it was when our servicemen and their allies asked me to represent them on the insignia for their units!

USS *Carson City*
San Francisco, California

USS *Yo 73*
Albina Engine & Machine Works
Portland, Oregon

Edward T. Dickens
London, England

1st Polish Divisional Signals
London, England

Through the pages of a storybook, we showed young readers the importance of buying war savings stamps. Kids all across the U.S. helped the war effort in a big way.

Goofy tried to show commuters ways to combat the shortages of rubber and gasoline—with the usual impractical but hilarious results.

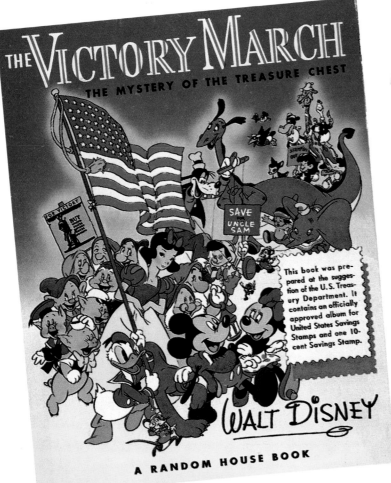

All of us at the Studio joined our government's good neighbor policy by extending the hand of friendship to our neighbors in South America.

...who decided to come back home with us. He still makes us laugh when he rolls himself up in a ball.

During one trip to South America, Pluto and I met a curious armor-plated armadillo...

Pluto and the Armadillo, 1943

My pals pitched in wherever they saw a need to help the war effort.

Pluto enlisted for a brief stint in the Army.

SHARE YOUR CAR

IT'S PATRIOTIC

Poor Pluto! He didn't seem to be too happy to help Minnie practice her first aid skills.

In order to save gas and wear and tear on several cars, we all carpooled to the Studio and encouraged others to do the same. Say! That message is as practical today as it was back then!

At the war's end in 1945, we could congratulate our friends and allies on a job well done and look forward to a return to a normal lifestyle. Of course, as Minnie would point out, for us "normal" never means "quiet and uneventful!"

In 1946, Pluto and I ran into Chip and Dale in a mountain cabin. I'm glad those little scamps later chose Donald as the object of their mischief-making!

Squatter's Rights, 1946

I got all duded up one night for a date with Minnie!

But one mishap after another left me looking...just right! I had forgotten I was supposed to be in costume.

Mickey's Delayed Date, 1947

What a surprise! Once I found a playful seal in my bathtub! Pluto wanted to chase him right back to the zoo!

Mickey and the Seal, 1948

In 1947, Donald and Goofy joined me in my second feature film. Here is our version of "Jack and the Beanstalk" from *Fun and Fancy Free*.

We played poor farmers with one pitiful bean to split three ways...

...until I traded our cow for some magic beans that grew into an enormous beanstalk.

At the top of the beanstalk we found a world where we were as tiny as insects.

I guess when you're a little guy, most of your problems are going to be bigger than you. But why did they have to be this BIG!

Fun and Fancy Free, 1947

37

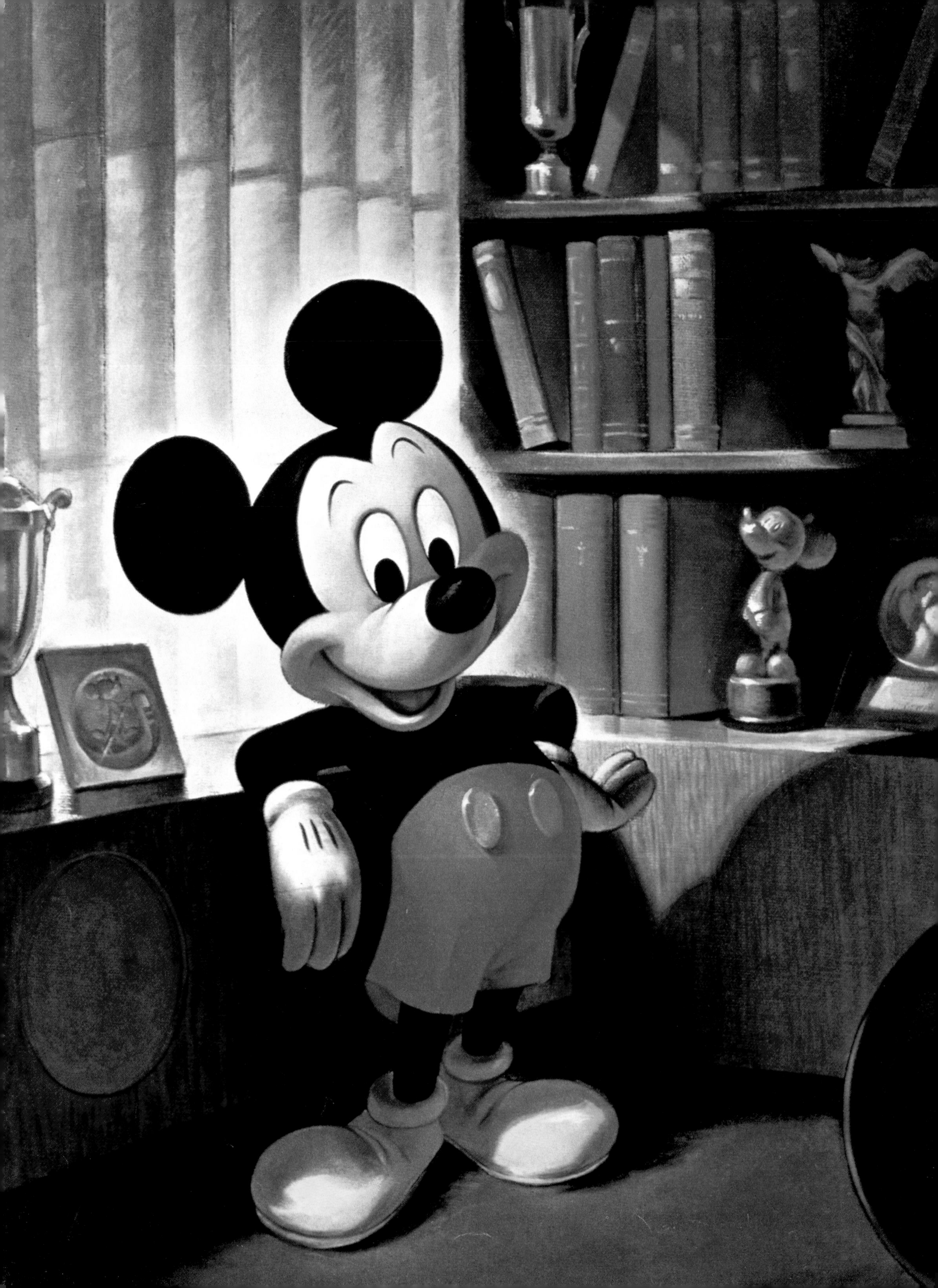

I had been making fewer and fewer films—the right roles just weren't coming my way. I thought maybe it was a sign that I should retire. You know—just sorta relax and take life easy. But unknown to me, Walt had even bigger plans in store!

My films and published adventures had made me friends all around the world. Now Walt gave me my own television show: *The Mickey Mouse Club.* Five days a week I marched from the TV screen into millions of homes. Kids all across the country greeted me with a wave of their hats (their mouse-eared hats, naturally), and joined in singing that catchy M-I-C-K-E-Y M-O-U-S-E theme song written especially for the show by my good friend Jimmie Dodd.

And if that wasn't enough to keep me busy, Walt opened Disneyland Park in Anaheim, California. I finally got a chance to meet my pals from all around the world in person.

Roy Williams created those famous "ears" worn by the Mouseketeers.

This official portrait was painted by John Hench for my 25th Birthday in 1953.

As I traveled around the world, I was surprised to find out that my friends in the countries I visited had their own special names for me.

In China's Mandarin dialect I'm called MI LAO SHU.

In Colombia I'm greeted as RATON MIGUELITO.

My friends in Finland say MIKKI HIIRI.

In France it's just plain MICKEY.

My German friends call out MICKY MAUS.

In Hungary I'm known as MIKI EGER.

In Indonesia my name is MIKI TIKUS.

In Italy I'm TOPOLINO.

In Norway I'm known as MIKKE MUS.

In South Africa I'm called MIEKIE.

In Sweden my pals call me MUSSE PIGG.

And in Yugoslavia I'm MIKI MAUS.

But no matter what name I'm given, it's called out with smiles and laughter. And that's a language understood all over the world!

ミッキーマウス

Micky Maus

R'coon Dawg, 1951

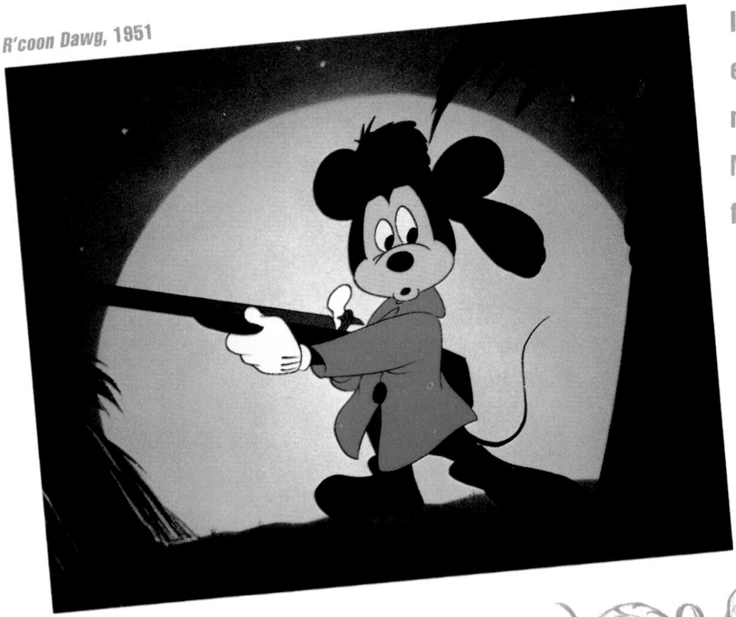

I was wearing a coonskin cap even before Davy Crockett made them a craze. And Minnie claims I have no fashion sense!

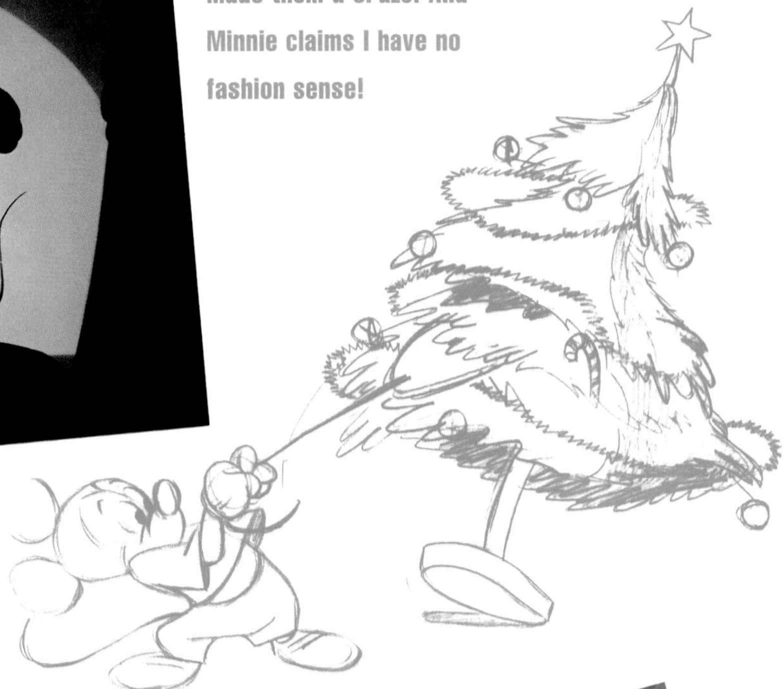

Surprise visitors are always welcome during the holidays...

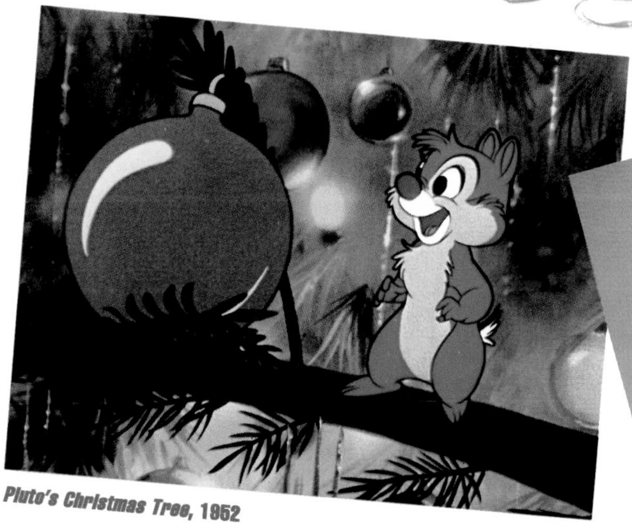

Pluto's Christmas Tree, 1952

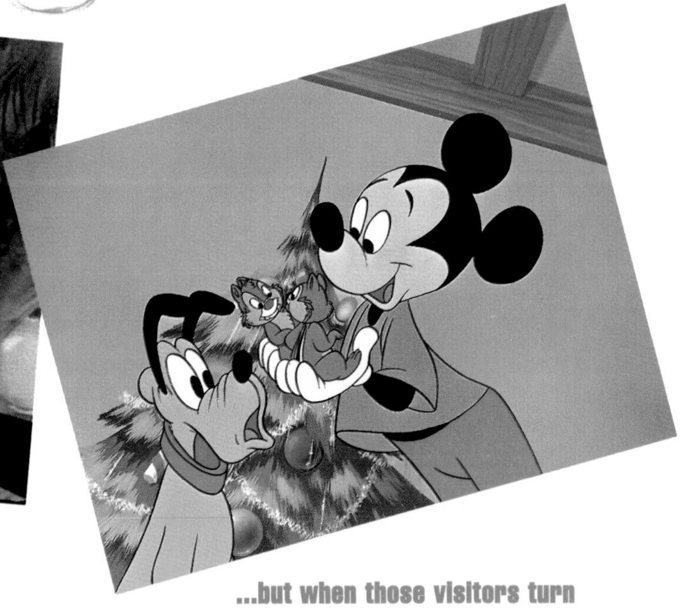

...but when those visitors turn out to be Chip and Dale, well, the surprises could fill Santa's sleigh!

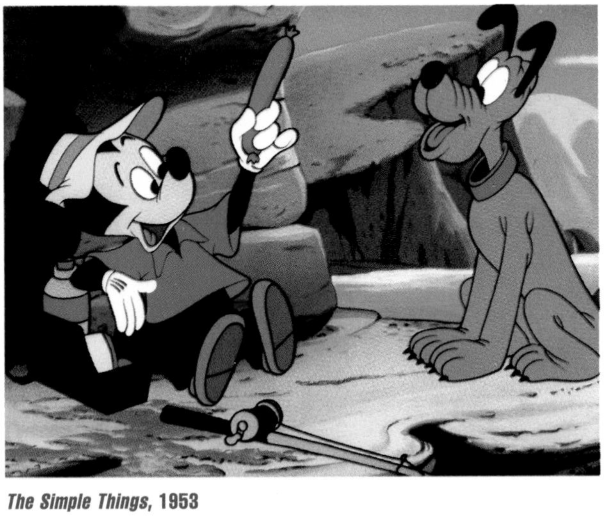

The Simple Things, 1953

It seemed as if my last movie of the '50s, about a day spent fishing, was pointing me toward a quieter lifestyle. I never suspected that in just two short years I'd be busier than ever!

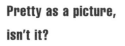

Pretty as a picture,
isn't it?

Walt and I walked through Sleeping Beauty Castle.

Here's Walt and me getting ready to chug into Main Street Railroad Station during the grand opening ceremonies for Disneyland on July 17, 1955.

Walt had my face planted in flowers at the entrance to Disneyland. He wanted my wide smile to welcome all the visitors to his Magic Kingdom.

43

Come along and join the jamboree! *The Mickey Mouse Club* premiered on October 3, 1955. And just like my original theatrical cartoons, folks watched us in glorious black and white. (Those were the days before color television.)

Naturally, we were in color on the movie-set side of the cameras.

Count on Donald to guarantee that each day's show started with a bang!

Every day on *The Mickey Mouse Club*, I greeted all my pals and set the stage for the day's program. Each day of the show had a theme.

Monday

Monday was "Fun with Music Day"—a natural for me, since I've had so much fun with music throughout my career.

Tuesday was "Guest Star Day," with visits from such favorites as Ed Wynn and Jerry Colonna, Olympic ice skating medalist Donna Atwood, Cliff Edwards (famous as Ukulele Ike), and Disneyland "balloon man" Wally Boag.

Tuesday

Wednesday

Wednesday was "Anything Can Happen Day"—and it usually did!

Thursday

Thursday was "Circus Day," complete with acrobats, clowns, and a menagerie of performing animals.

Friday

Friday was "Talent Roundup Day." Gee, it was fun watching the talented boys and girls from all over the country perform for our TV audience.

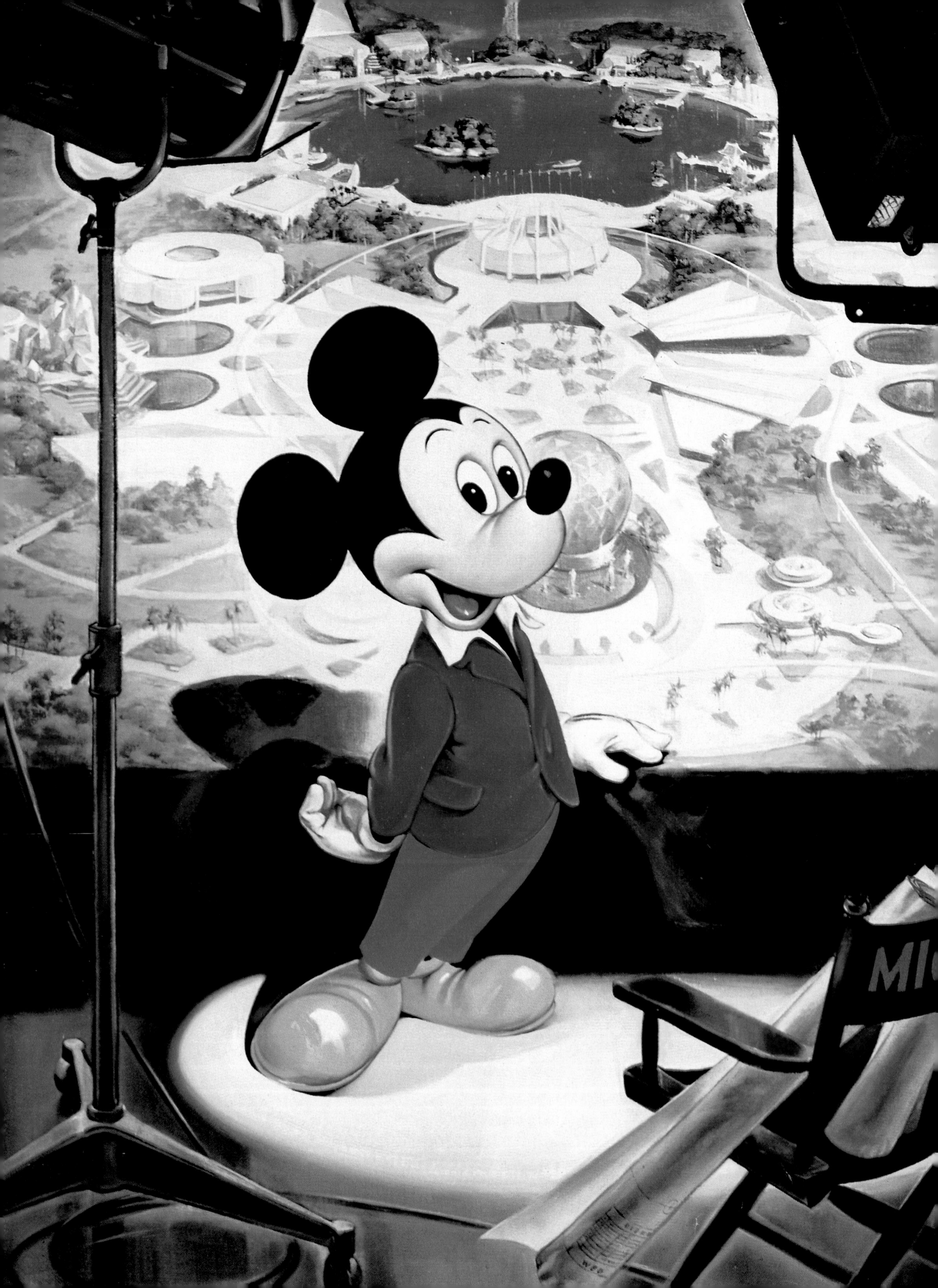

1960s & 1970s

People around the world shared our grief. A French magazine illustrated our loss simply but touchingly.

Once again John Hench painted my official portrait —this time for my 50th Birthday! I posed in front of the model for EPCOT—Walt's dream kept alive and continuing to grow.

Through the years I often made personal appearances with Walt Disney. Sometimes the event was a special Disneyland holiday parade or the premiere of one of our company's films. And sometimes I helped Walt introduce his latest dream—something he and his staff would create that would bring pleasure to young and old.

In the early '60s Walt, his brother Roy, and I traveled to Florida where Walt unveiled the plans for his biggest and most ambitious project: Walt Disney World and EPCOT. Little did we imagine on that exciting day that Walt wouldn't be with us to see that dream become a reality. My good friend died on December 15, 1966.

Working alongside Walt all those years, I learned one thing: dreams don't die. They grow and inspire. Roy Disney and the dedicated men and women in our company kept Walt's dream alive. On October 1, 1971, we welcomed the first happy visitors to the Walt Disney World Magic Kingdom.

When Walt Disney World opened in Florida on October 1, 1971, the gang and I packed our bags and were there as part of the celebration.

Just as at Disneyland, my face in flowers greets all the Walt Disney World Magic Kingdom visitors. I can't even guess how many millions of folks have had their photos taken in front of this colorful scene.

I even got to wave a conductor's baton again in one of the Park's original shows—*The Mickey Mouse Revue.*

In 1971, Ward Kimball produced a TV series showcasing our treasury of animated films and bursting with his unique sense of fun. In honor of me and the Studio where we both worked together, he called it *The Mouse Factory*.

Here's the cover for the original 1930 sheet music.

During each show I performed a funny dance to a version of the song "Minnie's Yoo-Hoo." That song was the first ever written for a Disney film, and for many years was the theme at the beginning of all my cartoons. What makes it very special for me is the fact that it was composed by Walt Disney and Carl Stalling.

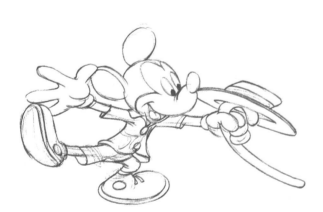

In 1978, I expected that I'd celebrate my 50th birthday kinda quietly, with just a few close friends. Well, that never happened! It seemed as if everyone in the world grabbed this opportunity to honor me in some way and let me know how much I meant to them. All that attention sure made me blush—more than once! But it also made me smile with happiness and gratitude.

In honor of my 50th birthday, Ward Kimball and I visited folks across the country, traveling on a special train.

Here's another of my official portraits—this one created for my 50th birthday by artist Paul Wenzel.

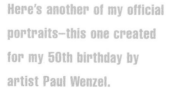

On November 3, 1978, I was given my star on the Hollywood Walk of Fame—the first actor in animated films to be so honored.

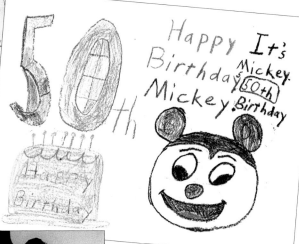

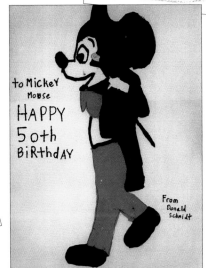

Golly, you should have seen all the cards sent to me by my pals from all around the world! Here are just a few of them. Aren't they swell?

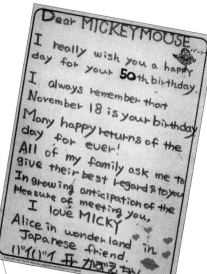

I'll never feel old when so many great kids make me feel young!

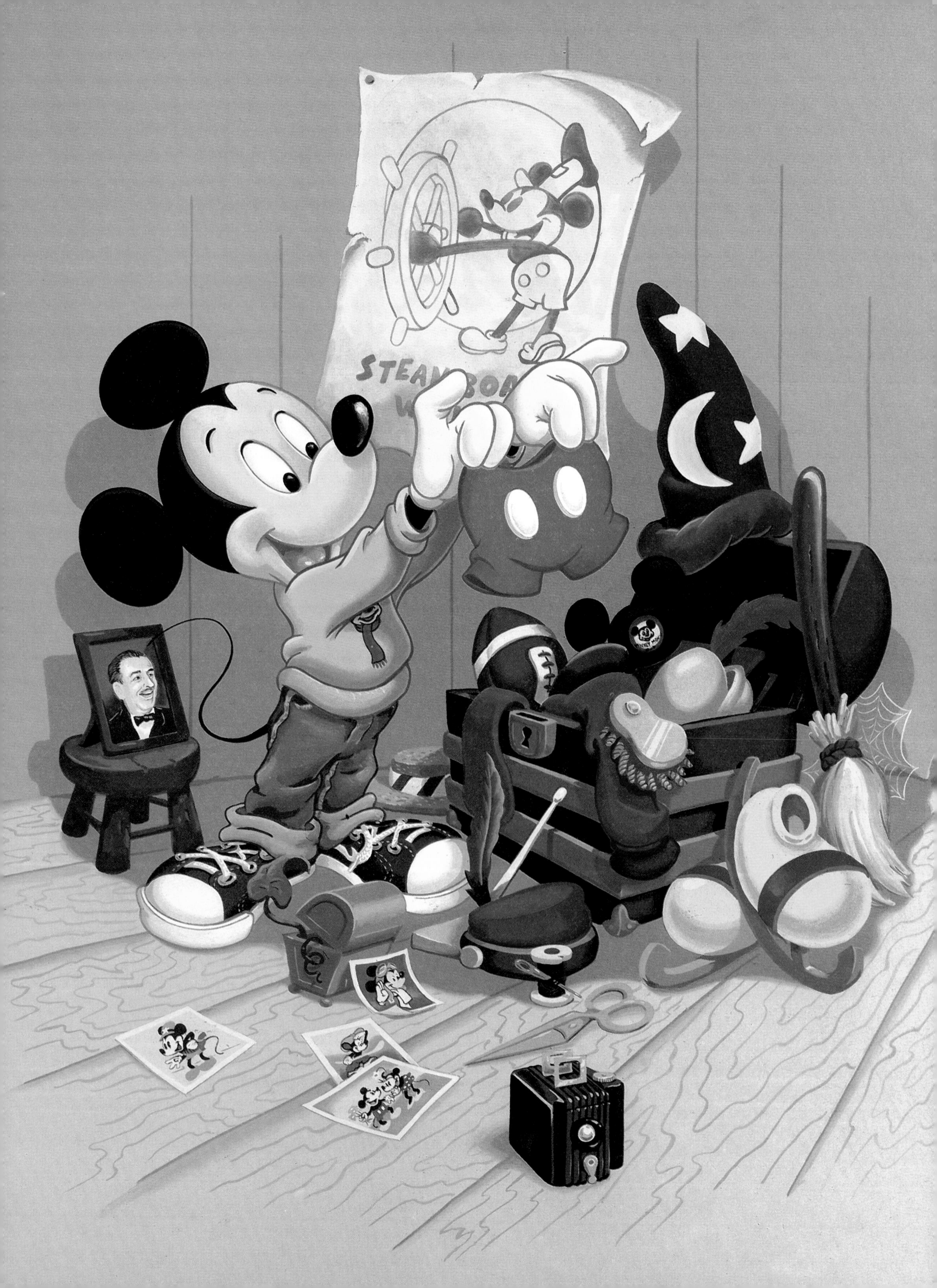

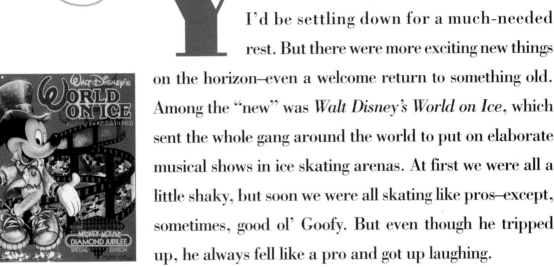

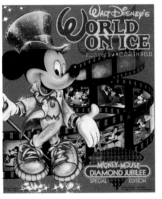

Walt Disney's World on Ice program.

The Disney Channel produced a poster for my 60th birthday in 1988. They asked me to pose with some of the mementos of my career. Boy, what memories! And soon I would be adding more.

Y ou'd think that by the time the '80s began I'd be settling down for a much-needed rest. But there were more exciting new things on the horizon–even a welcome return to something old. Among the "new" was *Walt Disney's World on Ice*, which sent the whole gang around the world to put on elaborate musical shows in ice skating arenas. At first we were all a little shaky, but soon we were all skating like pros–except, sometimes, good ol' Goofy. But even though he tripped up, he always fell like a pro and got up laughing.

What was the "old" thing that I began again? I started making movies once more! The first film was *Mickey's Christmas Carol* in 1983, my first in thirty years. And I've continued to appear in front of the cameras right into the '90s. I don't think I want to retire, after all!

The whole gang tackled a classic when we put together our own version of Charles Dickens's *A Christmas Carol.*

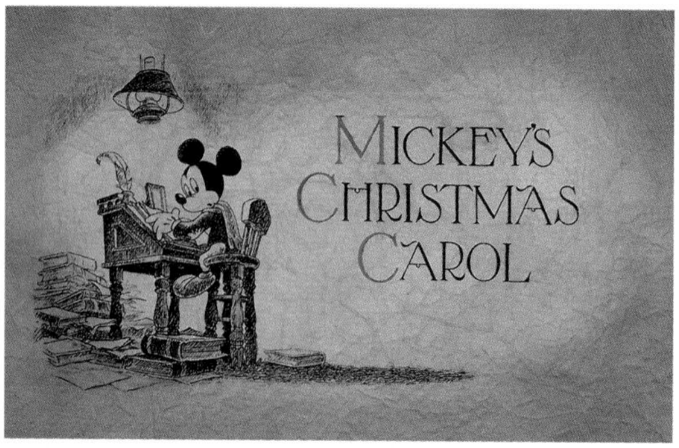
MICKEY'S
CHRISTMAS
CAROL

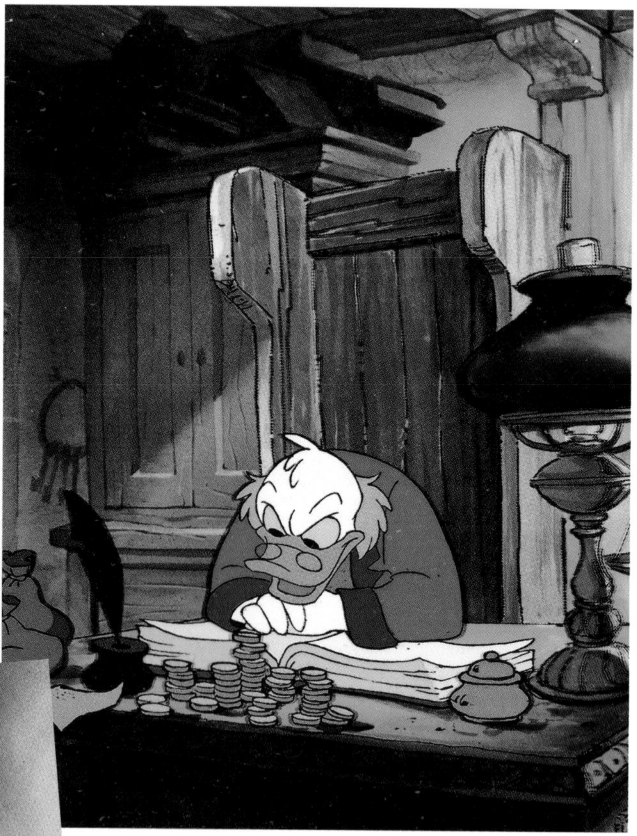

I played Bob Cratchit and Minnie played his wife.

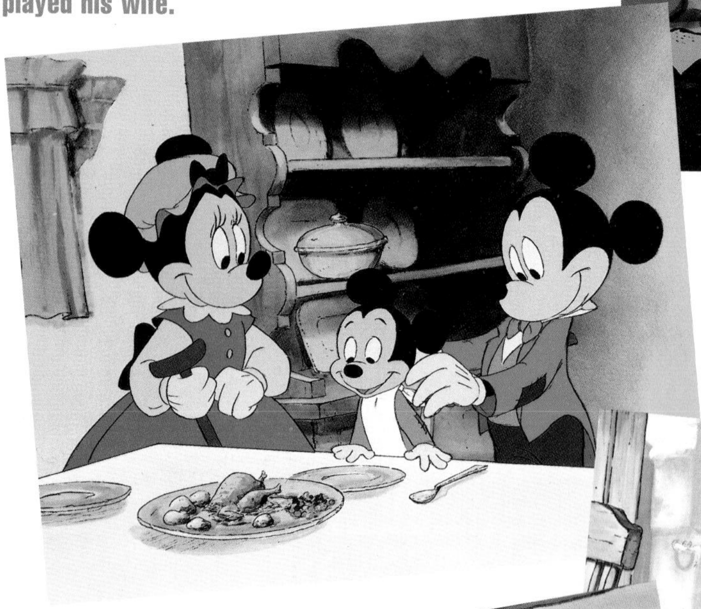

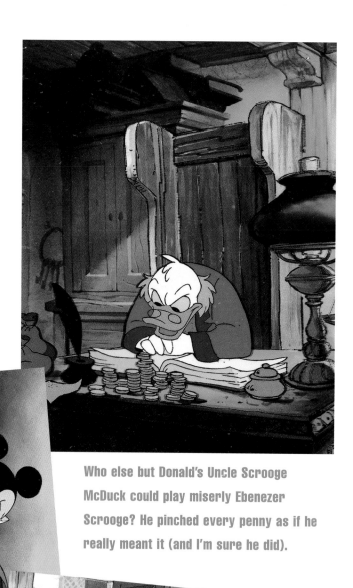

Who else but Donald's Uncle Scrooge McDuck could play miserly Ebenezer Scrooge? He pinched every penny as if he really meant it (and I'm sure he did).

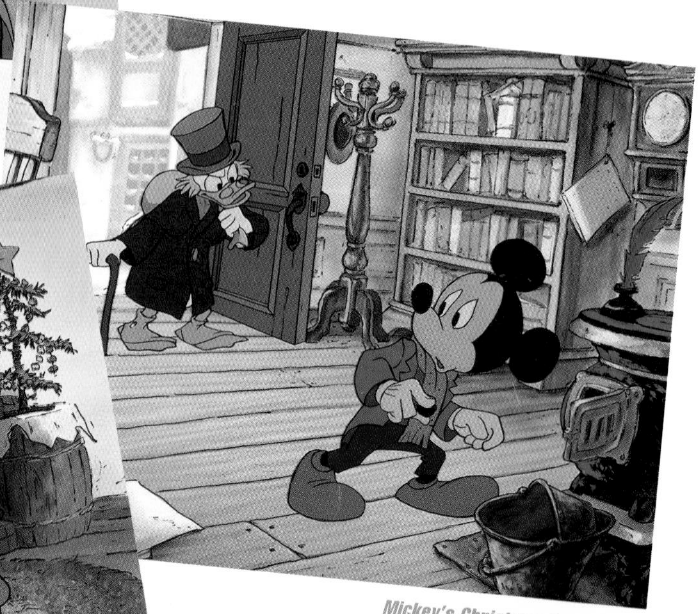

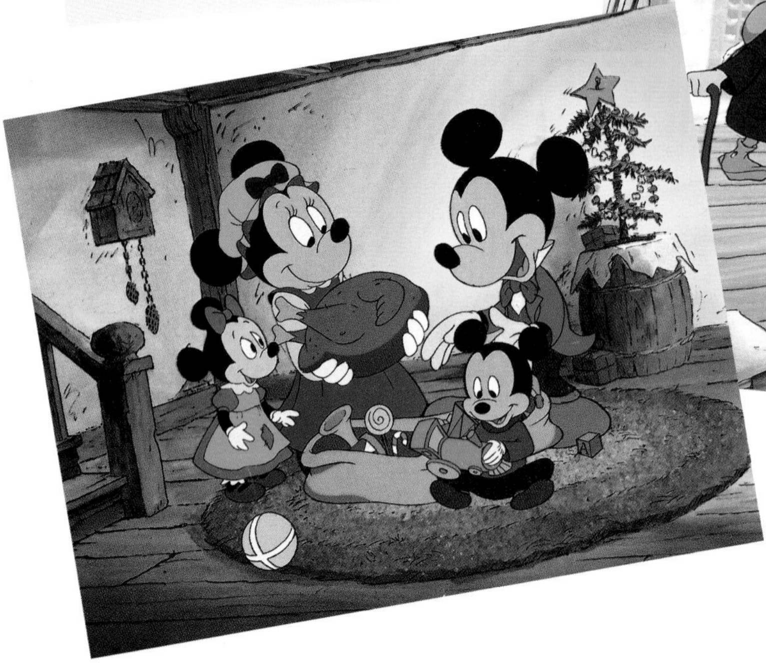

Mickey's Christmas Carol, 1983

Once, on the way to view some movie previews at the Studio theater we attracted a familiar following.

Sometimes I meet with Michael Eisner to discuss our upcoming films.

Sculptor Perry Russ created this statue of me. It greets visitors as they head down Hollywood Boulevard at the Disney-MGM Studios.

57

The Prince and the Pauper, 1990

A bit of movie magic enabled me to play a dual role in our 1990 retelling of Mark Twain's *The Prince and the Pauper*. Once again my friends showed their acting skills by appearing in costarring roles.

Greetings from Disneyland! Park visitors get a chance to come right into our homes in Mickey's Toontown.

A brand-new building for Walt Disney Feature Animation opened in December 1994. A new generation of animators passes under a giant-size version of my sorcerer's hat on their way to work. I wonder if it makes their stacks of drawings multiply as fast as my water-carrying brooms did?

59

My first short cartoon in forty years, *Runaway Brain*, premiered in 1995. It all started one dark and stormy night...

Runaway Brain, 1995

...when Minnie got upset with me because I had forgotten our anniversary.

Pluto helped me find a job in the want ads so I could take Minnie on a vacation to Hawaii.

But when I answered the ad, I fell into the clutches of the mad Doctor Frankenollie...

...whose evil experiment switched my brain with the brain of the monster Julius.

A Mouse with a monster's brain ran wild through the city.

Unaware of what had happened, Minnie tried to flee with the Monster Mouse.

Luckily, a freak accident switched our brains back to normal, but not before Julius got poor Minnie in his clutches.

To the rescue!

Sailing off into the sunset, we are towed to our vacation by a tamed Julius.

In 1993, a statue of Walt Disney and me was placed in the Hub at
the end of Main Street at Disneyland. Created by sculptor Blaine
Gibson, it's the permanent symbol of a friendship and partnership
that began on a train ride from New York back in 1928. And
more importantly, it tells us that when you believe in your
dreams, anything is possible.

We've been playing and working together for almost seventy years now, and we're still the best of friends. It's great to look back on all the fun we've been a part of, but there's nothing to match the excitement of the future and the surprises to come. And with my good friends by my side to share the adventure, who could ask for more?

I get to say thanks!

Putting this book together was made so much easier and just plain fun thanks to the help I received from some really special folks:

Becky Cline, Collette Espino, Shelly Graham, Andrea Recendez, Dave Smith, Ed Squair, and Robert Tieman at The Walt Disney Archives; Ann Hansen and Larry Ishino at The Walt Disney Animation Research Library; John Loter and Laura Zinkan at Consumer Products Licensing; John Dreyer at Corporate Communications; Jeff Leavitt at Corporate Graphics; Maria Josey at The Disney Channel; Debbie Barlow at The Disneyland Photo Dept.; James Bice at Park Films; Margaret Adamic at Disney Publishing; Debi Dooley at the Disney Publishing Reference Library; Eric Huang, Thomas S. Phong, and Jeanette Steiner at Publishing Creative Development; Zoë Gangemi at Walt Disney Feature Animation Communications; Amy Cox, Mike Jusko, Diane Scoglio, and Randy Webster at Walt Disney Imagineering; Mark Seppala at Walt Disney World Attractions Merchandise; Teri Hayt at The Walt Disney World Photo Dept.; and my editor at Disney Press, Howard Reeves.

To all my countless coworkers who have supported me throughout my career with your love, dedication, and talents: you've kept a smile on my face and a twinkle in my eye. You're the best!

And to my fans and friends from all around the world–well, all I can say is this: I wish you as much joy and happiness as you've given me. You've been my greatest blessing. I'm one lucky guy!

Mickey Mouse
Burbank, CA
February 4, 1997